TALKING IT THROUGH

My Stepfamily

Rosemary Stones

Illustrated by Heather Dickinson

Happy Cat Books

When my mum told me she had a new boyfriend she wanted me to meet, I was excited but also a bit nervous. I wondered whether he'd like me. I told mum I wanted to wear my new dress and my stripey socks when he came round. She said I looked fine as I was but then she said OK.

I thought Tim was nice. We drove to the Natural History Museum and looked at the dinosaurs. Some of them must have been bigger than a house. He told me he has a daughter too. Her name is Clare and she is younger than me.

My mum and dad got divorced when I was a baby so I was glad to see mum happy with Tim. He started staying with us a lot. Mum was pleased I liked him too.

Then mum said Tim was going to bring Clare with him next time he came. I thought Clare would like to see my Barbie doll and my bike and my den in the garden. Mum and me bought fruit yoghurts, a raspberry one for me and a peach one for her.

But it wasn't a nice afternoon. Clare didn't like her fruit yoghurt and she didn't want to play in the den. She put the wrong clothes on Barbie and she creased the pages of my best book. She kept saying, "Daddy! Daddy! Where's my daddy?" She was silly.

Then Tim and Clare moved in with mum and me.
The very worst thing was that I had to share my
bedroom with Clare. That meant there was no room
for my wardrobe. It had to go on the landing and I had
to make room for Clare to have half for her clothes.

Mum said it would be like having a
little sister. I said, "I don't want a little
sister." Mum sighed and looked cross.

The first few weeks Clare kept waking up in the night and crying. Tim had to come in to give her a cuddle. Mum and Tim got very tired and fed up. When I asked if I could have my friends from school round for tea they said no. It was all Clare's fault. She was such a baby.

And when I went off to play on my own Clare kept following me shouting, "Kim! Where are you? Can I play, Kim? Daddy! Kim won't let me play."

She wouldn't leave me alone.

Mum said I had to be nice to her because I was the oldest.

Once Tim got cross with me for hitting Clare when she took my Barbie without asking. She got away with all sorts of things I wasn't allowed to do. It wasn't fair.

When Tim wasn't there, mum let Clare have all her own
way. I had to watch baby programmes on the TV instead
of what I wanted.

Everything was all right until Tim and Clare moved in.
I thought perhaps mum didn't want me now that she
had a new family.

Then it was my birthday. We were going to drive to a big park where there are deer and have a picnic.

But in the car Clare started whining. She wanted her baby story tape instead of the one I wanted. I felt so fed up I didn't say anything but I thought, "Nothing is going to be nice ever again. Not even my birthday."

To my surprise, mum said, "No, Clare. Kim's the birthday girl. She chooses which tape."

Clare started crying to get her own way but then Tim said, "No, Clare! Kim is going to choose."

So we had the story of The Three Little Pigs and
we all joined in with the huffing and puffing.

When we got to the park I had to say where to have the picnic. I found a nice place under a great big tree and we watched the deer while we had our sandwiches. Then there was a surprise birthday cake with candles and my name in pink icing.

Clare and I went off to explore while mum
and Tim sat and read the papers. That's when
we met the horrid girls.

They had a big dog which ran up to Clare
and barked at her and ran round and round
her in circles.

Clare was scared and started crying. The girls began laughing at her. "Who's the silly crybaby?" one of them said. "This nasty doggy's hungry," said the other. "He's going to eat you all up!"

I was so cross I shouted, "Don't you be horrid to my sister! She's only little." I took Clare's hand and we ran back to mum and Tim.

"Daddy! Daddy! Daddy! Kim stopped the horrid girls," said Clare. "They had a nasty dog who was going to eat me all up."

"Well done, Kim!" said Tim.

"Just like a real big sister!" said mum.

Now things are better at home.

Although there are four of us, mum and me still have our special times together.

Kim can be a nuisance sometimes but now it's hard to imagine not having a little sister.